You're a
disgrace, Daisy!

Also in the Definitely Daisy series:

You're a disgrace, Daisy!

Jenny Oldfield

Illustrated by
Lauren Child

Hodder
Children's
Books

a division of Hodder Headline Limited

For Alex and Mia

First published in Great Britain in 2001
by Hodder Children's Books

A Catalogue record for this book is available from
the British Library

ISBN 0 340 78498 9

Printed and bound in Great Britain

Hodder Children's Books
a division of Hodder Headline Ltd
338 Euston Road
London NW1 3BH

One

'Daisy Morelli, watch out for the wet... paint! Oh dear!'

Miss Ambler's warning came too late. Daisy had reached over the art table for a clean brush and smudged Winona's beautiful picture.

'Please, Miss, Daisy spoiled my sunflower!' Winona wailed.

The teacher came across the classroom to

inspect the damage.

'I know she did, dear. And she ruined her nice clean school shirt as well.'

Daisy stared down at the yellow paint on her chest. Then she wiped her sticky hand on her dark grey skirt.

'Don't do that, Daisy!' Miss Ambler shrieked.

Too late again. Daisy's skirt now matched her shirt. *So what?* she thought. *Paint washes off, doesn't it?*

All she'd wanted was a clean brush to start her own painting with. And now Winona was making this fuss about her stupid sunflower. Privately, Daisy felt the flower looked better now than it did before, with a nice, artistic handprint right in the middle.

'Miss, I'll have to start all over again!' Winona whinged.

Miss Ambler comforted her star pupil. 'Never mind, dear. Why don't you tidy up and then help me take down the old pictures from the wall? Daisy Morelli, you can stay in during playtime and scrub the art table for being so careless.'

Winona's whinge changed to a smug smile. She tossed her long, fair curls at a scowling Daisy. 'Serves you right!' she whispered.

'What did I do?' Daisy asked, turning to her best friend, Jimmy Black.

Jimmy carried on sploshing yellow paint across his paper. *Sploosh – sploosh – dabble – dabble – splosh*!

Daisy forgot her troubles with smarmy

Winona. 'Hey, that doesn't look anything *like* what it's supposed to look like!'

Splosh – sploosh – squiggle – stab! Jimmy painted on.

'It's more like a custard pie than a sunflower!'

Squiggle – squiggle. 'Don't care!' Jimmy replied.

Miss Ambler came by with a small metal stepladder, closely followed by Winona. 'Very nice, Jimmy dear,' she murmured. Then the teacher frowned hard and told Daisy off again. 'Come away from Jimmy's table, Daisy Morelli. If I've told you once, I've told you a thousand times; don't interfere with other people's work!'

'Daisy, leave Nathan's spider jar alone!'

Playtime had come and gone. Scrubbing the art table had added red, blue and green splodges to the yellow stains on Daisy's shirt and skirt. And missing the playtime soccer challenge had put her in a really bad mood.

'We won, four-nil!' Jimmy had whispered, as he slid into the seat next to Daisy's. His face was red and sweaty, his football shirt ripped at the shoulder. But he was happy.

'Don't tell me, I don't want to know!' Daisy had moaned, giving Winona the dead eye.

And now it was Science, and she was in trouble with Miss Ambler again.

All she'd done was take a pencil and get ready to poke Legs, the fat black spider Nathan Moss kept as a pet. Winona Smarmy Jones had watched her do it, then run off to report her to the teacher.

'I'm not even touching him!' Daisy pleaded her innocence and hid the pencil behind her back.

'Miss, she nearly did!' Winona claimed. 'I saw Legs trying to run away and hide!'

How could a spider hide in an empty jam-jar? Daisy scowled at Winona, the teacher's pet. Mizz Neat-and-Petite, with her golden curls and ironed shirts.

And now Nathan came and whisked his precious spider to safety. 'I hope he escapes from his jar and gives you a poison-bite!' he hissed.

Weird Nathan who never bothered to tie his shoe laces. Nathan who knew everything about spiders and nothing about football. Like, seriously weird!

Daisy refused to be scared. 'Legs doesn't bite. He's cute.'

'Yuck!' Winona whispered to her curly-haired neighbour, Leonie Flowers. 'Daisy thinks creepy Legs is cute!'

Leonie carried on with her amazing drawing of a spider's web. The thin black lines formed a neat network on the white page. 'Me too,' she murmured. 'He's all soft and furry...'

So Winona flounced off to join Nathan. And Daisy stayed in Miss Ambler's bad books.

One hour later, Daisy was out of the classroom on a mission.

'Come away from that pond!' A loud voice made her jump. She staggered, tottered, then stepped into the shallow water.

Mr King, the school caretaker, came rushing up. His pet bulldog, Fat Lennox, panted along behind him. 'I said, mind you don't fall in!' he cried. Too late again.

'Miss Ambler sent me to collect pond-weed for our Science lesson,' she explained. The teacher's idea had been to give Daisy a job to do to keep her out of trouble. Only, here she was, getting told off again.

Squelch! When she lifted her foot out of the pond and put it down on the grass, her trainer oozed muddy water.

Bernie King took no notice of Daisy's lame excuse. 'A likely story!' he fumed, looming large, keys to every door in the school hanging in a bunch from his belt. 'No teacher with a grain of sense would send you on a tricky errand like that!' The caretaker didn't like Daisy. Or Jimmy, or Leonie – in fact, he was probably in the wrong job, since he frankly didn't like kids, full-stop.

Daisy backed away. She forgot that the pond was behind her. Only when she stumbled into the weeds and mud again, then sat down in the cold water with a bump, did she remember where she was.

'Didn't I try to warn you?' King grunted. 'I said, stay away from that pond!'

Daisy stared down at her own sorry figure. She was wet. Her shoes were muddy.

Her clothes were covered in paint. This had
not been a good day.

'Daisy, don't you dare go near the baby
looking like that!'

Angie Morelli waited at the school gates
for her daughter. She gasped in horror as
Daisy ran to paw her chubby little sister with
muddy, paint-smeared hands.

'Aah, goo-goo-goo! Chobble-chobble,
wibble-wobble!' Winona Jones was there
first, poking her nose in and cooing over
Mia's push-chair. She picked up a pink
stuffed rabbit from the pavement and
handed it back, goo-gooing and choo-
chooing all over again.

'Goo-goo-goo!' Mia chortled back.

Meanwhile, Jimmy and Leonie sped by.

'Race you to the bus-stop!' Leonie
challenged.

Jimmy nodded, took the corner with a
screech of pretend-brakes, then legged it
down the street. Daisy bet herself five

pounds that Jimmy, who could run like a whippet, would win the race.

'Daisy, you're a disgrace,' Angie grumbled wearily. 'What did I do to deserve a daughter like you?'

'"Daisy, you're a disgrace!"' Daisy mimicked behind her mum's back, while Angie sighed, then turned to talk to another mother.

Winona stepped in smartly. 'I *saw* that!' she hissed.

'So?' Daisy was fed-up. She'd had enough. More than enough. Too much, in fact. So she jutted out her chin and faced up to Win-oh-stupid-nah. 'What you gonna do about it?'

'Daisy, don't argue!' Angie Morelli said sharply, glancing over her shoulder.

"Daisy – Daisy – Daisy – don't – don't – don't!" First from Miss Rambler-Ambler and Bernie King. Now from her mum. "Don't do that, Daisy. Daisy, you're a disgrace!" She was sick of it.

So sick that she would... she would... well, she might even explode. Right here, right now, on this pavement. She fizzed and sparked inside, fidgeting and feeling the pressure build up.

'Daisy, what's wrong? Why has your face gone a funny colour?' Winona asked sweetly.

Mia tossed her pink rabbit out of the push-chair again. No one told *her* off.

'It's not fair!' Daisy fumed. She watched Jimmy arrive at the bus-stop ten metres ahead of Leonie, noted that she had just won five pounds from herself; a sum of money which anyway she didn't have.

'Why is it always me?'

'Because it always *is* you!' Winona replied with deadly logic. 'I mean, face it, Daisy, if there's trouble around, you're going to be in the thick of it! Like, *definitely!*'

Definitely Daisy pulled a sour face and stuck out her tongue.

'Daisy, that's not nice!' (Her mum had eyes in the back of her head, of course.)

'It's true!' Winona insisted. Then she wormed her way into Mrs Morelli's conversation and invited herself to the Morellis' house for tea.

No, not that! Anything but that! Daisy pleaded silently for her mum to say no.

'Of course. Daisy would love to have you, wouldn't you, Daisy?' Angie said, a steely eye fixed on her squirming daughter.

Oh no! Get me out of here! Daisy gave Winona a furious look as the small group set off down the street. *Aliens, please land in your spaceship and kidnap me! Beam me off into another dimension, take me to a distant universe. Only, please, please, don't leave me here on Woodbridge Road and make me have tea with girly, curly, pearly Winona (Call-Me-Mizz-Perfect) Jones!*

Two

'Hello, my *bambino*!' Gianni Morelli lifted Mia out of her push-chair and held her high in the air. The baby giggled and gurgled. She wiggled her fat arms and legs like a frog.

'Bambino Mia. Mia bambino!' The proud dad laughed and tossed the baby. Then he took her off into the kitchen, where he was busy cooking pizzas.

Daisy and Mia's dad ran an Italian

restaurant on Duke Street called the Pizza Palazzo. He was always laughing, always tossing the baby into the air.

These days he seemed not to notice Daisy.

'Put your school bag away in your room,' her mum told her, once Winona had gobbled up a whole pizza margarita, drunk three large Cokes and waddled off home. 'Your dad will be cross if you leave it lying around in the restaurant.'

Daisy frowned. She knew for a fact that her smiley-faced dad had never been cross in his life. He just laughed his way through the days, pounding pizza-dough, chopping onions and dreaming of Italy.

'And put your school uniform in the washing-machine.' Angie Morelli continued to nag Daisy. 'How come you got into such a state at school today? Honestly, Daisy, why can't you be neat and tidy like Winona?'

Daisy waited until her mum had left the room, then stuck two fingers down her throat and made a puking sound.

'You feeling OK?' Just at that moment, Jimmy popped his head around the door. His dark brown hair was blown about by the wind, his blue football shirt was covered in mud and he held a white plastic ball under his arm.

'No!' Daisy retorted.

'Oh.' Jimmy turned to go. 'I was gonna ask if you wanted to come and play footie with us in the park...'

'Wait!' Daisy's amazing recovery surprised her friend. She shot out on to Duke Street, still in her paint-spattered uniform. 'Who's playing? Whose side am I on?'

'Goal!' The cry went up from Jimmy's team as he slammed the ball into the back of the net. 'Jim-my Black! Jim-my Black!' Jimmy did a tour of the pitch, his arms in the air, allowing his team mates to slap him on the back.

'Two-one!' Daisy cried. They were five minutes into extra time after a hard-fought one-all draw. Part of the winning team, she galloped after Jimmy and flung both arms

around his neck.

'Gerroff!' he protested, ducking, then elbowing her away.

She didn't care. She was happy and hot, sweaty and chanting, 'Jim-my Black!'

Their team held on to the lead in spite of Leonie's two brave efforts to level the score.

'Oooh-aaah!' Her team mates gasped, then groaned as her second shot went wide.

Leonie collapsed on to her knees in disappointment. She held her head in her hands.

Then the final whistle blew and it was all over.

'Good match!' Jimmy trotted around the pitch, which was marked out with rolled-up jackets and spare shoes. He congratulated his team and shook hands with the gallant losers. 'Bad luck, Leonie,' he muttered.

'We'll hammer you next time!' she promised, running a hand through her short curly hair, then glancing at her watch. 'Gotta go. My mum will kill me!'

And so the players went their separate ways in the setting sun, and Jimmy and Daisy walked back home to Duke Street together.

'Have you done your Science homework for tomorrow?' Jimmy asked, stopping outside his family's flat, which was above Car World, the motor spares shop.

'Nope,' Daisy replied. Homework was boring. Homework was for wimps like weird Nathan.

'Miss Ambler will kill you.'

'Don't care.' She wandered on ten yards to the Pizza Palazzo.

'Daisy Morelli, didn't I tell you to put your uniform in the wash...?' her mum began as soon as she set foot through the sliding-doors.

OK, so the alien spaceship hadn't landed and come to her rescue. So she was walking to school next morning without her Science project. 'Please, Miss, the baby chewed it!' was going to be her excuse. The teacher would never believe her, but so what?

'She'll make you stay behind to do extra work,' Jimmy warned, waving his own dog-eared project in her face. Somehow, the hero of last night's soccer match had also found time to write out the life cycle of the newt.

'So?' Daisy unhitched the hem of her newly-ironed shirt from the waistband of her skirt. A headline on the billboard outside the newsagents caught her eye: "LOCAL HERO TO SET UP KIDS' SOCCER ACADEMY!" 'Hey, look at this!'

Jimmy saw it too, then grabbed a copy of the Helston Herald from the pile. 'It says here that Kevin Crowe is starting a football school for the under-twelves. If you're chosen, you get to live in and learn soccer skills from the greatest goal-scorer in the Steelers history!'

'Wow!' To Daisy this sounded too good to be true.

'Hey, you kids, put that paper down!' the newsagent yelled from inside the shop.

'Picture it!' Jimmy sighed as they walked on to school.

'Kevin Crowe is only a living football legend, that's all!'

Daisy's head was still full of the idea of the soccer school when Miss Ambler took off her glasses and groaned at her feeble excuse for not handing in her homework.

The young teacher rubbed her eyes wearily. She got up from behind her desk, snagged a thread from her flared cotton skirt on a splinter and pulled the hem loose. 'Ttt-ttt!' Her tongue clicked against her front teeth and she frowned down at her least favourite pupil. 'Daisy Morelli, you're a complete disgrace!'

'Yes, Miss Ambler.'

'Do you really expect me to believe that poor little Mia ate your homework?'

'No, Miss Ambler.'

'I should think not. This may only be my first year in teaching, but even I can spot a fake excuse when I hear one.'

Silence this time from Daisy, as she

awaited her fate.

'I'm afraid you've gone too far.' Miss Ambler trembled in front of the whole class. Her voice quivered. 'I intend to speak to the head teacher about you at playtime. Unless I'm very much mistaken, Daisy Morelli, Mrs Waymann will definitely want to have a little word.'

It was morning break. For once, Daisy didn't join in with the soccer-playing gang. Instead, she daydreamed in a corner of the yard.

"...And it's Daisy Morelli surging down the middle! She's dribbled past one defender, now another... this girl's ball skills are truly superb!" The presenter's voice rose as Daisy headed for the goalmouth. *"Yes, she's drawn the goalkeeper out, she's flicked the ball past him and now she's shooting with that famous left foot... Slam, into the corner of the net!"*

It was the winning goal of the FA Cup final. Wembley roared. Fans spilled on to the pitch. After the match, the presenter interviewed her.

"So, Daisy, tell us, who's behind your soccer success story?"

Blushing, Daisy thanked her mother and father, her friend, Jimmy Black, and most of all, the great Kevin Crowe.

"I understand that you attended his famous Academy for the Under-Twelves?" The presenter reminded twenty million TV viewers of Daisy Morelli's footballing roots.

She beamed at the camera, then spoke. 'Yeah, thank you, Kevin. Without you, I'd be a footballing nobody..."

'Waymann wants a word,' Leonie dashed up to break into Daisy's dream and pass on a message. 'She says to go to her office right now.'

Daisy nodded. Hands behind her back, head down and heart thumping, she made her way into school.

Up the steps to the executioner's block. "Do you have any final requests?" "Yes. Tell my mum and dad I'm sorry." Whoosh! The axe descended as Daisy knocked on Mrs Waymann's door.

'Enter!' The head teacher's voice sounded stern.

Daisy shuffled in.

Mrs Waymann looked up from writing reports, her plump face serious. She shifted her weight, giving off a cloud of flowery perfume. 'Ah yes, Daisy Morelli. Miss Ambler would like me to have a little word...'

'What did she say?' Jimmy quizzed Daisy on their way home from school.

It was Friday; the end of the worst week in Daisy's life.

Pull-yourself-together. Smarten-up. Tell-the-truth. Daisy gave Jimmy the lowdown on her lousy interview with the head teacher. Oh, and, '*You simply must stop living in a fantasy world.*' Plus, '*Daisy Morelli, you're a headache.*' And, '*Daisy, you attract trouble like a magnet.*'

Mrs Waymann might *look* plump and cuddly sitting in her cloud of perfume, but appearances weren't always what they seemed.

'Daisy-Disaster-Morelli' was what she'd called her, before finally deciding that there was no way around it; she, Mrs Waymann, would be obliged to write to Daisy's parents about their daughter's poor behaviour in school.

'Phew, bad news!' Jimmy whistled. 'What you gonna do?'

'Run away from home,' Daisy told him,

matter of factly. She'd already got it all planned out in her head.

'Are you serious?' Jimmy's jaw nearly hit the pavement.

'Where are you gonna run to?'

'It's a secret.'

'Yeah, but you can tell me. I'm Jimmy, remember; your best mate!'

Daisy relented. 'OK, I'm planning to pack my bag in the middle of the night tonight. I'm gonna write Mum and Dad a note, saying not to worry, I'm safe and all that. Then tomorrow, before breakfast, I'm gonna creep out of the house without anyone seeing.' As she described her secret plan, her dark eyes sparkled. This was going to be one BIG adventure.

'Yeah, but where to?' Jimmy insisted. They had reached Duke Street and his mum was standing, arms folded, at the door of Car World, looking out for him.

'That's the really good bit,' Daisy whispered. 'The plan is, I sneak off from here and get in touch with Kevin Crowe.'

The famous name stopped Jimmy dead in his tracks. '*The* Kevin Crowe?' he stammered.

She nodded.

'What on earth for?' said a flabbergasted Jimmy.

'I want to join his Academy.' To Daisy it all made perfect sense. 'I'll learn to be a soccer superstar, and then, when I'm scoring the winning goal in the World Cup Final, everyone who ever nagged me or told me off will have to be sorry!'

'Yeah!' Jimmy's glance was admiring at first. Then he hit a serious snag, which he felt he had to point out. 'But you're a girl!'

'Yeah. So?'

'Girls don't play in the World Cup. They don't even play in the League.'

A deep frown creased Daisy's forehead. 'They soon will!' she promised. She would prove herself so gifted at heading the ball that Kevin Crowe would go along to the FA and get them to change the rules.

Jimmy took this on board. For a while he

rolled his eyes thoughtfully. 'The Kevin Crowe Academy for Under-Twelves,' he muttered. Then he chucked in a casual suggestion. 'How about I run away too? I could come with you to the Academy.'

Daisy looked him in the eye. 'Seriously?'

'Jimmy, come in for your tea!' his mum called from the doorstep. 'It's bangers, chips and beans!'

Jimmy ignored her, his eyes alive with excitement. 'Truth!' he swore.

'OK!' Daisy said, swiftly making up her mind. 'Meet me tomorrow morning at the park gates, eight o'clock sharp!'

Three

No more school.

No more Miss Ambler shrieking, 'Daisy, you're a disgrace!' No more miserable Bernie King jangling his keys, shaking his head and saying, 'Sorry, no can do!'

Curled up in bed that night, Daisy thought of all the things she wouldn't miss.

No more homework – cool. And none of that naggy stuff from the dinner ladies about washing your hands before you ate your dinner.

Hey, and no more tidying her classroom drawer!

Uh-oh! Suddenly Daisy gasped, then sat bolt upright in bed. She'd just remembered Herbie.

Herbie was her squidgy, furry golden hamster and she'd left him behind in her drawer. Not just for the weekend, as it happened, but forever.

'What's the matter, love? Why aren't you asleep?' Daisy's mum poked her head around the bedroom door.

'I forgot Herbie!' she wailed. He would be lonely and scared in that dark drawer, amongst her broken crayons and crumpled worksheets.

Angie Morelli smiled. 'Is that all? I thought it was something serious.'

'It is! I never leave Herbie behind. He doesn't like being by himself.'

'Hmm.' Daisy's mum came to sit on the

edge of the bed. 'You don't think you're making a bit too much of this? Herbie isn't a real hamster, remember. He's only a soft toy.'

'Only!' Daisy squeaked. 'I've had him since I was little!'

OK, so he was half-bald and squidgy from going through the washing-machine too many times. And maybe he did only have one eye and these days his colour wasn't exactly golden. But, uncool as it sounded, Herbie was still her special hamster. And the closest Daisy had ever come to a real live pet.

'Do you know where you left him?' Angie asked kindly.

'In my drawer.'

'That's OK, then. He'll still be there on Monday.'

But I won't! Daisy frowned, then slid back down under her duvet to hide her face. She mustn't let her mum suspect what she and Jimmy were planning.

'Better now?'

'Mm.' (Close eyes, pretend to be sleepy.)

'Good. Sleep well.' Angie stood up and tiptoed out. 'Good night, Daisy!'

No reply from the hump in the bed. Daisy produced a couple of loud snores for effect. She heard the light switch on the landing flick off and her mum's footsteps go quietly downstairs.

'Listen, Jimmy, we have to go to school!'

Daisy's announcement at eight o'clock next morning came as a shock. 'B-b-but!' he stammered. 'It's Saturday. Anyway, I thought we were running away!'

'We are. It's just I need to fetch Herbie.'

'Fetch Herbie?' Jimmy echoed. He shifted his half-empty rucksack from one shoulder to the other. The bag contained only a spare football kit, a toothbrush and a signed photo of Robbie Exley, the Steelers' ace goal scorer. 'Do we have to?'

Daisy nodded. 'Think of the one thing

you would never leave behind...' She
waited for him to suggest something.

'My Robbie Exley pic.' There was no
doubt in Jimmy's mind. He'd rather die
than be separated from Super-Rob.

'Right. So you'd go back to school to
collect him if you'd left him behind,
wouldn't you?' she asked with a piercing
look.

'OK.' He gave in and agreed to head for
Woodbridge Road, still coming up with
reasons not to as they drew near. 'It's not
a week day. What if school's locked?'

'It won't be. There's a netball match.
They have to open the building so kids can
use the changing-rooms.' Daisy had
thought all this through during the night.
And poor Herbie had been at the front of
her mind all the time she was secretly
packing and saying goodbye to sleeping
baby Mia.

Goodbye, Mi-mi! Goodbye, bedroom!
Goodbye, Mum and Dad (who had been

busy stacking shelves in the restaurant store-room.) Then finally, *Goodbye, Pizza Palazzo!*

That had been the tough bit; knowing that you would never see your home and family again. Or at least, not until you became a sporting hero and returned in triumph on the open topped, Cup-winners double-decker bus.

Daisy had slid out of the door on to the street, her bag on her back, her heart heavy. She'd even shed a tear over Mia and slipped a passport-sized photograph of herself under the baby's pillow so that Mia wouldn't forget her older sister. Then she'd propped the farewell note to her parents against the microwave and beaten a hasty retreat.

Maybe Jimmy won't show up, she thought, as she nipped around the side of Car World and headed for their meeting place at the park gates. In which case, I could change my mind about running away to Kevin Crowe's Football Academy after all.

But Jimmy was already there in his newest bright blue football strip which was a little bit too big.

So she had to go through with the plan. But, before they set off to look for Kevin Crowe's place, she had to rescue Herbie.

'We'll have to sneak in without being seen,' Jimmy whispered as the school gates came into view.

'Yoo-hoo, Jimmy! Yoo-hoo, Daisy!' Winona Jones called from across the street.

She was taking her fancy pet poodle, Lulu, for a walk. The curly-haired white dog trotted along beside her neat owner, ears pricked, pom-pom tail poked straight up in the air.

'Ohhh... no!' Daisy and Jimmy groaned.

Winona and Lulu crossed the street to join them. 'I didn't know you played netball, Jimmy!' she joked.

'Ha-ha,' he said crossly.

'Very funny,' Daisy chipped in.

'So what are you two doing here?'

Winona eyed their rucksacks suspiciously.

Quick-thinking Daisy gave the reply. 'We came to watch Leonie.'

'You're loads too early.' Glancing at her watch, Winona made it clear that she thought they were up to something.

'Yeah, we're here to help make the orange juice and biscuits for half-time,' Jimmy lied, his freckled face burning bright red.

'Hey, me too!' Winona sounded pleased that she wasn't the only helper.

Trust Mizz Perfect, Mizz Teacher's Pet to offer to help Miss Ambler on a non-school day. Daisy cringed.

Winona was positively bubbling with excitement. 'Wait here for me while I take Lulu home, OK? I'll only be five minutes. Then we can all go into school together.'

So Jimmy and Daisy stood by helplessly while Winona scooted off down the road. But as soon as she turned the corner, they zoomed across the empty playground towards the main door.

'See, it's locked!' Jimmy sighed after he'd rattled and turned the handle in vain.

'Sshh, here comes Bernie!' Daisy spotted the stout figure of the caretaker crossing the yard from his house. His keys jangled as usual, and he was armed with a metal bucket full of steaming water plus a long-handled mop. Fat Lennox followed close behind.

Daisy and Jimmy ducked down behind two giant flower tubs until Bernie and his bulldog had passed by.

'I dunno, kids these days!' he grumbled to himself. 'They don't know they're born. They have it too easy; someone to drive them to school, someone to drive them home again. In my day you had to walk, come rain, come shine...' He muttered on as he put down his mop and bucket by the entrance. Then he gave a loud sigh as he unhooked his keys to open the door.

From behind her flower tub, Daisy gave Jimmy a thumbs-up signal. In a few seconds, after they'd given the caretaker time to stomp off down the corridor, she and Jimmy would be able to sneak in after him.

'In my day, you did a paper-round before breakfast, then you walked into school,' Bernie reminded himself. 'Kids today are too soft by half...'

Jimmy and Daisy watched him pick up his clanking bucket and go on his way. Then they darted into the school, past the Welcome board outside the secretary's office, and down the corridor into their own classroom.

Once inside, Daisy dived straight for her drawer. She pulled it out and rummaged amongst the rubbish, spilling felt-tips down the back and throwing her history project on castles on to the floor. At last she found what she was looking for.

'Herbie!' she cried, pulling out a squished, dirty-brown soft toy.

The hamster's one remaining eye seemed to wink at her as she brought him out into the light.

'C'mon, Daisy, let's get out of here!' Jimmy urged from the doorway. 'I can hear Bernie coming back!'

Clank-clank-clank went Bernie King's bucket. His keys *chink-chinked* as he walked.

So she stuffed Herbie into her bag and sprinted with Jimmy back down the corridor before the caretaker had time to reappear.

'Close!' Jimmy breathed.

'Yoo-hoo, you two!' a voice called from the gate.

'Oh no!' Daisy had forgotten about Winona. She screeched to a halt and looked for a different way out of the playground.

'I thought you said you'd wait for me,' Winona protested, making a neat run to cut off their retreat.

'That's not the way I remember it!' Jimmy said darkly.

(*Reasons to hate Winona Jones*; Daisy made a list.

One: *Because she's always neat and curly-girly.*

Two: *Because she's a teacher's pet.*

Three: *Because she owns Lulu, a real live pet, not just a toy.*

Four: *Because she always asks stupid questions...*)

'What have you got in that bag, Daisy? Why didn't you wait like you said? And Jimmy, what are you doing helping out at a netball match instead of playing footie in the park?'

Daisy was still looking for an escape. But now the side exit was blocked by the arrival of Miss Ambler's rattling, rusting orange VW Beetle. The teacher had obviously shown up on her day off to take charge of the girls' netball match. Worse still, Winona was nipping across the playground to speak to her.

'Please, Miss, Daisy Morelli and Jimmy Black are going to help me with the refreshments!' she announced in a loud voice.

A startled Miss Ambler almost dropped the pile of netball shirts she was carrying. 'That's news to me,' she said with a quick glance at the shifty pair.

'Quick!' Daisy hissed. She'd decided that the best way out of this emergency was over the playground wall.

She and Jimmy shinned up it and were balanced on the top when Bernie King stormed out of the school.

'Hey you!' The caretaker steamrollered towards them, arms waving, voice raised to a bellow. Fat Lennox barked behind him.

'Get down off that wall before you do yourselves an injury!'

While Daisy judged the five foot drop on to the pavement below, Jimmy took off. He landed commando-style, rolling on to his side, then springing on to his feet. 'All clear!' he yelled back at Daisy, still teetering on top of the wall. So she jumped to join him.

Crouching low, bags bumping against their backs, they skirted the playground, back towards busy Woodbridge Road.

'What now?' Jimmy hissed, pinning himself against the wall as he reached the corner.

'We catch a bus into town and start looking for the Kevin Crowe Academy.' Daisy formed her plan on the spur of the moment. After all, it couldn't be hard. Everyone would have heard about the new soccer school, so all she and Jimmy needed to do was ask at the Information Office for directions. *Easy-peasy.*

'I heard that!' Winona's voice broke in.

Swivelling round, Daisy spotted the enemy crouched on the wall directly above their heads. Winona was wearing her smug, wait-till-I-tell-Miss-Ambler expression.

'So?' Jimmy answered back. 'What's wrong with us looking for the Kevin Cro... *ouch*!'

Daisy had stamped hard on his toes and was glaring at him.

Up on the wall-top, Winona's eyes narrowed. 'You two are running away, aren't you?'

'No way!' Daisy snapped.

'Definitely not!' Jimmy held his foot and hopped about.

'You are!' Winona crowed.

Daisy reached up and caught hold of her ankle. 'Don't you dare say a word!'

Winona wobbled and squeaked. 'OK!'

Daisy tugged harder. 'Promise?'

'Promise!' Winona gasped.

Giving her one last glare, Daisy let go. Winona sank back into the playground, out of sight.

Jimmy spotted a number seven bus pulling up at the nearby stop and they sprinted to catch it. Forget Winona, Miss Ambler and Bernie King. Think about the Kevin Crowe Academy and the adventure about to begin!

Four

The trouble with running away from home was that you soon got homesick, Daisy discovered.

Not that she would admit that to Jimmy, who sat quietly beside her on the front seat of the top deck of the number seven bus.

Don't be so silly! she told herself, sounding strangely like Miss Ambler. It's only half an hour since you left the note in front of

the microwave. Mum and Dad won't even
have had time to miss you yet!

Dear Mum and Dad,
I've had ~~enff~~ enough. I'm always
getting told off and I can't take it
any more. So ~~I've~~ I've decided to
run away. Please let the school know
that I won't be coming in any more.
Mrs Waymann called me Daisy Disaster
Morelli so she should be pleased.
The same with miss Ambler (please
tell her that I did __not__ Poke Legs
and I'd never do anything to hurt
him. I LiKE SPiDErS!!!)
And don't try to look ~~for it~~ me.
Just show mia my picture and tell
her about me when she grows up.
your loving ~~dort~~ daughter, Daisy
PS. I'm doing this totally alone,
by myself, just me. no one is coming
with me !!!

As the bus rumbled and lurched through the Saturday morning traffic, she remembered word for word the letter she had written.

'Whassamatter?' Jimmy mumbled when he heard Daisy sniffle.

'Nothing!'

'Are we on the right bus?'

'Yep.' *Sniff-sniff-swallow.*

'Sure?' He sat tensely on the edge of his seat, looking down at City Road.

'Sure I'm sure. There's the Steelers' ground, see.' Daisy pointed out the famous stadium lights two streets away. Highfield had been the city's home ground for more than fifty years; a meeting place for football fans everywhere.

Jimmy saw the ground and fell quiet. Perhaps he was dreaming of the goal he would score for the Steelers at Highfield one day. *His power-packed right foot would pile the ball into the back of the net and the League title would be theirs...*

Meanwhile, the bus shuddered to a halt to let on more passengers.

Daisy glanced down and recognised a familiar, untidy figure in the queue. 'Oh no!' she groaned. How unlucky could you be when you set out to run away? First Winona, now Nathan!

There was no mistaking Nathan Moss. There was only one boy in the world whose faded fair hair stuck out at weird angles like that, whose glasses were always mended by tape, and whose shoelaces were always undone...

'Hey, Jimmy. Hey, Daisy,' Nathan muttered as he climbed the stairs. He sat down in the seat behind them, dumping the trumpet case he was carrying on the floor between his feet. Then he got out a small plastic wallet and carefully slid his yellow bus ticket into one of the slots, alongside a pink one, a blue one and a boring beige one.

'I collect them,' he explained to Daisy. 'Every time I go to Music Centre for my trumpet lesson, I use a new route so I can buy a different colour ticket.'

Like, wow! she thought. But at least Nathan was too weird to wonder what she and Jimmy were up to. She hoped.

'How's Legs?' she asked, to divert attention from the bulky rucksack beside her.

'Legs is fine,' Nathan replied. Then, 'What have you got in that bag?'

'Dirty washing,' Daisy said, quick as a flash. 'Our washing machine broke down, so I have to take it to the laundrette.'

'Hmm.' Nathan spotted Jimmy's similar bag. 'How about you?'

'Same thing.' Jimmy coloured up straight away.

He was a terrible liar, Daisy knew. And he didn't seem to be happy with the way their running-away plan was working out. In fact, she'd never known Jimmy to be so quiet and stiff; most unlike his usual self.

Nathan frowned. 'Don't you think that's a really interesting coincidence?' he said. 'Seeing as you two live next door to one another and both your washing machines have broken down at the same time?'

Was he joking? Daisy stared hard at Nathan's pale face and electric-shock hair. Nope, he seemed deadly serious. He really *was* deep into working out the chances of two Zanussis on the same street breaking down together.

'Sorry, Nathan, this is our stop!' Jumping up from the seat, Daisy dragged Jimmy down the aisle.

Slowly Nathan turned his head. 'Hey, Daisy!' he called, glasses glinting in the sunlight. 'I expect you don't want me to mention that I saw you?'

'Yeah... I mean, no... I mean, yeah, don't
say anything!' she stammered.

She jumped off the bus ahead of Jimmy,
then glanced up to see Nathan still staring
gleefully down at them from his high seat.
And she could have sworn he winked.

'Is it that obvious?' Daisy muttered, striding
through a crowd of pigeons pecking grain in
Fountain Square. 'I mean, do we look like two
kids who are running away from home?'

Jimmy ran to keep up. 'Yeah,' he told her.
'We do.'

Pigeons flapped and flew off in all
directions as Daisy and Jimmy charged
through their midst.

'Hey you!' an old man with a bag of pigeon-
food yelled. 'Walk, don't run!' The fat grey birds
wheeled overhead and swooped down again.
Peck-peck-peck at the food, *waddle-waddle*
towards the man in the old shell-suit.

Jimmy and Daisy slowed down. They came
to a halt by the steps to the Central Library.

'What are we looking for?' Jimmy asked.

'The Information Office, to ask about the Academy,' she reminded him.

'Don't just stand there!' A woman pushing twins in a wide pushchair complained that they were blocking her way.

Jimmy and Daisy scuttled clear. Then Jimmy spotted a blue sign with a white 'i', plus an arrow pointing across the square. 'Over there!' he cried.

He led the charge back through the flock of over-fed pigeons, up on to the low wall surrounding the tall fountain, along the brim, getting splashed to bits. 'Yeah!' he yelled wildly as the icy water spattered down.

'I'm wet through!' Daisy cried. Hair, T-shirt, rucksack; everything.

'Get down from that wall, you two!' a man in a bright yellow plastic jacket cried; a council worker employed to clean up the square after the pigeons.

Miserable spoilsport! Daisy groaned and jumped down, squelching after Jimmy, who

always seemed to run faster, balance better,
kick the ball further than anyone else she knew.

They arrived at the Information Office out
of breath and dripping wet.

'Close that door!' The woman behind the
desk looked up as soon as they walked in.

She was as grey and over-fed as the pigeons, with her dull hair frizzed out in a perm. 'And don't slop water over my nice clean floor!'

Don't – don't – don't! It seemed to Daisy that she could never escape that dreaded word.

The Information Officer carried on glaring at her two new customers. 'Stay there. Don't move until you've drip-dried!' she instructed.

Jimmy stood by the door in his wet football strip, his teeth chattering, knobbly knees knocking. He stared around at the rows of maps and leaflets, the posters on the walls, the shiny souvenirs on the counter. 'P-p-please...' he began.

'Wait a moment, I'm busy!' the woman snapped, disappearing from behind her desk into a back room.

Daisy pulled a face. All they wanted to do was ask a simple question.

So they waited. And dripped. And waited.

Outside, the sunlight reached the fountain and lit up a million sparkling drops. More people crossed the square with shopping bags, pushing bicycles and pushchairs. A man with a guitar and a thin brown dog set out a collection box and began to play.

The fat grey woman peered out from her inner room. 'Still here?' she snapped at Jimmy and Daisy before she vanished again.

In the warmth of the sun Daisy felt her T-shirt begin to steam. It was time to wander across to one of the racks of leaflets, flick through, and try to find one about the Kevin Crowe Academy.

So she and Jimmy shuffled towards the sports and leisure section. They spotted a leaflet for the steam railway, the swimming-pool, the ice-skating rink, but nothing for the new soccer school.

'Don't mess up my display!' Mizz Frizz returned to catch them fingering the leaflets in her precious rack.

Jimmy and Daisy cowered back. Then Daisy gathered her courage. She walked firmly towards the desk. 'We'd like some information, please.'

'What *kind* of information?' the woman grumped.

'Sport and leisure. We're looking for a leaflet –'

'I can see that. I'm not blind.'

'– on the new soccer school for under-twelves run by the ex-Steelers goalkeeper, Kevin Crowe,' Daisy gabbled.

'Huh, then you're wasting your time.' The Information Officer sounded pleased that she was unable to help. Her chins wobbled as she shook her head and told them that there was no such leaflet in print.

'How come?' Jimmy asked, a worried look creeping on to his face.

'Because there's no such school.'

'But it was in the paper. We read about it!' Daisy felt a shockwave run through her body. What did she mean, "no such school"?

'Yeah, Kevin Crowe is running a live-in Soccer Academy for talented youngsters!' Jimmy recalled the newspaper piece word for word. 'We're going to join!'

The chins wobbled, the little beady eyes

disappeared behind a fat smile. 'Dream on, sonny!'

"Dream on"? Daisy gripped the edge of the desk. 'What are you saying? Why can't we join the school?'

The woman smiled down at them and delivered the all-important piece of information that Jimmy and Daisy had both missed in the newspaper.

'Because it isn't open yet,' she told them. 'In fact, they haven't even found a building, or got the money to set it up.'

No building? No money? No soccer school to run away to?

Daisy's dream plummeted to the ground like a dead pigeon.

'Come back next year,' the woman suggested. 'And mind you don't drip on my carpet as you leave!'

Five

Daisy pulled a damp Herbie out of her bag
and hugged him.

Jimmy stood in Fountain Square holding
back the tears. 'What now?' he asked.

*Now we'll never clinch the Cup for
Steelers. We'll be failures and we'll never
be able to go home in triumph...* All Daisy's
hopes were shattered.

'I mean, what-do-we-do-now?' Jimmy

gabbled, a look of panic in his eyes.

Buses and trucks roared around the Square, the man with the thin dog and the guitar wailed an unhappy song.

"Leavin' on a jet-plane
Don't know when I'll be back again
Oh, babe, I hate to go..."

The dog rested his chin on his front paws and whimpered.

Daisy looked up at the fountain, at millions of sparkling water drops, and failed to find an answer to Jimmy's desperate question.

'Do we go home?' he insisted.

Daisy pictured the scene. She would turn up on the doorstep of Pizza Palazzo with an embarrassed grin on her face. Her farewell letter would be open and lying flat on the table. Her mum would cry all over her and ask what she'd done to deserve a daughter like Daisy. Her dad would look disappointed and carry on sprinkling cheese on the pizzas.

'Can't!' she muttered to Jimmy. *Anything but that.*

'Why not?'

'Because...!'

OK, so the Kevin Crowe Academy didn't exist. So they couldn't return to Duke Street amidst clouds of footballing glory, but there must be something else they could do.

Jimmy's unhappy frown deepened. His bottom lip quivered.

Chink-chink, the coins dropped into the guitarist's collection box.

"So kiss me and smile for me...

Tell me that you'll wait for me..."

'Hmm-hmmm-mmm!' the dog whined and pricked up its ears. Then it lifted its head and caught a sudden movement behind the fountain. Two seconds later, it was on its feet and trotting to investigate.

'Hey, leave Legs alone!' a familiar voice cried.

'Nathan!' Jimmy and Daisy sprang into action. They skirted the fountain after the dog and came face to face with Nathan Moss and Winona Jones.

Nathan hastily popped his giant spider back into its jam-jar while Winona shooed the dog away. 'I told you to leave Legs inside his jar!' she said crossly. '*Now* look what happened!'

Nathan shrugged, then spotted an amazed Daisy and Jimmy. He gave them a weird smile. 'Don't blame me. It was her idea.'

'What are you doing here?' Daisy demanded. Couldn't Winona Jones, just for once in her life, leave her alone?

'Following you. It's OK, I asked permission from Miss Ambler. She got somebody else to do the orange juice and biscuits.'

'How about you?' Daisy asked Nathan. 'Why can't you mind your own business?'

'I just bumped into Winona outside Music Centre, and tracking you two down sounded amusing,' he explained, screwing the jam-jar lid down and perching Legs on the concrete rim surrounding the fountain.

'Yeah, hah-hah! Well done. Now that you

found us, what are you gonna do?' Daisy
stood with her hands on her hips. 'Sneak off
and tell Miss Ambler, why don't you? Go on,
get us into trouble, and it's not even a school
day!'

Winona frowned severely. 'Daisy, it's for
your own good. You can't just run away to a
soccer school...'

'Which doesn't even exist,' Nathan added
swiftly. Trust Nathan to have checked his
facts first.

'So, what's it to you?' For the first time
Jimmy joined in the argument. He stooped to
pat the bothersome dog, who'd come back
to join them carrying a chewed tennis ball in
its mouth. Jimmy took the ball and chucked it
straight into the water for the dog to fetch.

Woof! The thin brown dog jumped into the
sparkling fountain, retrieved the scraggy ball
and emerged from the water dripping wet.

'Yuck!' Winona screeched as the dog
shook itself dry. Her pretty pink shirt and
white trousers were drenched.

'Watch it!' Nathan warned. The dog almost knocked Legs' jam-jar from the ledge into the fountain. He scrabbled to catch it, like a cricketer fielding in the slips.

Daisy seized her chance. 'Run!' she yelled at Jimmy. No way were they going to stick around to be turned in by Winona and Nathan. No, the intention was to lose the enemy, then re-group.

So they ran.

Through the fountain, with the mad brown dog plunging after them. Across the square, up the library ramp, sploshing and dripping every step of the way. Through the sliding doors, leaving the dog behind and with no sign of Winona, Nathan or Legs in pursuit.

'This way!' Jimmy cried, running between rows of books.

Up the escalator to the art gallery, down a long, deserted room lined with portraits of women in big, hooped dresses and men in plumed hats on horseback. The gallery attendant woke up from her doze too late to

stop Daisy and Jimmy from using the
emergency exit.

Then down the stairs, out of the building
through a back door into a car park, dodging
between parked cars, nipping under a
striped barrier, legging it across the road to
the safety of the Marshway
Shopping Centre.

'Phew!' The flight had sent the blood rushing through Daisy's veins. Her heart thumped hard against her ribs. But now they were inside the glass-covered maze of shops, there was no chance of Winona and Nathan picking up their trail.

For a start, the place was crowded with Saturday shoppers.

OK, so kids stared at Daisy and Jimmy's dripping figures as they sped by McDonalds.

So the two of them looked like they were on the run, bumping into people with their bags, glancing over their shoulders every step of the way. But who cared?

They had lost Nathan and Winona. They came out the far side of Marshway with fresh hope.

'You still wanna know what I think we should do now?' Daisy demanded. She pushed her long, black-brown hair out of her eyes and squared her shoulders.

Jimmy nodded eagerly. He stood in front of an electrical goods shop window filled with fifty TV screens all playing the identical sports programme.

Football, football, football.

Teletext news about players who were injured, the latest mega-bucks transfers, the announcement of a new team coach to lead the Steelers to Premiership victory.

'Turn around and take a look!' Daisy invited him.

It was there on the screen; the news that

their team had appointed Kevin Crowe to replace Henri Argent, the coach who had left earlier in the week to return to his native France.

Kevin Crowe, all-time great goalie, local hero and now the new trainer at Highfield.

Fifty identical, smiling Kevin Crowe's stared down at Daisy and Jimmy from the TV screens. It was like a sign, a secret message telling them what they should do next.

'C'mon!' Daisy said, without spelling it out in full. 'If we move fast, we can reach the ground before Kevin arrives to greet the team!'

'Robbie, over here!'

'Robbie-Robbie-Robbie. Rob-Rob-Rob!'

'Sign this programme for me please, Robbie... oh, please!'

A hundred fans mobbed the star player at the players' clubhouse entrance.

Head down, Robbie Exley made his way through the crowd. His blond hair shone like corn stubble in the sunlight and there was a pleased smile on his handsome, square face.

'Jimmy, look who just arrived!' Daisy jabbed her friend with her elbow. 'Go ahead, get his autograph, before he disappears inside!'

But Jimmy was overcome, unable to move a muscle. He stood at the edge of the precious ground, catching a glimpse of his hero through dozens of yelling fans.

So Daisy acted for him.

She squeezed through to the front of the mob, bobbing under arms, sliding through narrow gaps and ending up next to the man himself.

Robbie was grinning as he signed a young fan's autograph book with a fat felt-tip.

'That's it!' he insisted, putting the top back on the pen. 'I'm out of time. Would you let me through?'

Daisy stood in his path, staring up at him. 'My friend Jimmy thinks you're the best soccer player in the world!'

'He does?' Robbie's grin widened. He looked down at a scruffy, determined, dark-haired kid. ('Robbie-Robbie-Robbie. Rob-Rob-Rob!')

She nodded. 'He wants to play like you one day.'

'So I'd better watch my back!' The superstar laughed and sidestepped Daisy.

She ran after him. 'Can he have your autograph?'

Robbie gave in and unscrewed the pen

top. 'Where's your autograph book?'

Oh no, no book. Not even a sheet of paper! So Daisy turned around and offered the back of her pale-blue T-shirt. 'Sign this!' she begged.

Robbie grinned again, then recited the words which he scrawled. 'To Jimmy – with best wishes to a star of the future. Yours, Robbie Exley.'

'Magic!' Jimmy whispered. He read the message on the back of Daisy's T-shirt.

'It's yours, Jimmy!' she promised. 'As soon as I get back home – no, as soon as I find something else to wear – you can have this T-shirt for keeps!'

Jimmy's eyes shone, a smile lit up his pointed, flushed face. It was like he'd died and gone to heaven. 'Thanks, Daisy!'

'Watch out, you two!' a fellow fan warned, as a swish silver car cruised towards the entrance.

Daisy and Jimmy squashed against the gate-post. They watched the passenger door swing open and the Steelers' new coach, Kevin Crowe, step out.

Kevin was dressed in a smart suit, blue shirt and dark blue tie with a Steelers' logo. His grey hair was cut short, his lean face tanned. He smiled and waved a hand as the cheers and good-luck calls of the gathered fans rang out.

Someone opened the player's entrance

door from the inside. 'The boss is a busy man. Let him through,' a voice ordered. But Daisy was flushed with her Robbie Exley success and she had no intention of missing this chance.

She and Jimmy were small. The door was wide, and an unruly bunch of autograph-hunters almost knocked down the doorman. So Daisy and Jimmy ducked to crawl between a few pairs of legs. Before they knew it, they were through the gate with their unwitting soccer hero.

Daisy was close enough to reach out and touch him. But was she brave enough to ask him the only question that mattered to her in the whole world?

Six

'Can Jimmy Black and me be your first pupils at the Under-Twelves' Soccer Academy?'

This was Daisy's fall-back plan, formed on the hoof as she and Jimmy ran away from nosey-parkers Winona and Nathan. She'd seen the item about Kevin Crowe's new job on the TV sport round-up, and decided there and then to put their names at the very top of the list. Once Kevin had accepted them as his first full-time pupils, all she and Jimmy had to do was stay in hiding for a year until the Academy opened its doors

'How do we hide for a whole year?' Jimmy had asked.

'Easy.' Firmly dismissing his doubts, Daisy had described how they would find a boarded-up flat near the football ground and become squatters. They would live there in secret.

'Are we old enough?'

'Jimmy!' She'd sighed and rolled her eyes. 'Do you want to do this, or not?'

He'd swallowed, nodded and tagged along. 'But what do we eat?' he'd wanted to know.

'Stuff,' Daisy had said. Like, *Don't bother me with small details.* Then, 'We can get paper-rounds to earn some money and buy Big Macs with.' Easy.

'Are we old enough?' Doggedly Jimmy pointed out the problems.

'We can pretend to be twelve, can't we?'

'OK, so how do we keep warm in winter? Do we tell our families where we are so they can lend us a heater?'

Daisy had despaired of answering his questions. 'Trust me,' she'd pleaded. 'All we have to do is speak to Kevin outside the players' entrance. After that, all the rest will fall into place!'

And here they were now. The doorman was still battling to shut the gate on the noisy fans, and the Greatest Goalkeeper of All Time was considering their request.

'Let me get this straight. You've sneaked in here after me in order to enrol in the junior soccer school when it opens?'

Daisy and Jimmy both nodded until their heads nearly fell off. 'We could be your very first signings,' Daisy pleaded. 'Jimmy's ace with his right foot, and I'm pretty good with my left.'

The corners of Kevin's mouth twitched. 'I admire your cheek,' he told them. Then he ordered the cross-looking doorman not to bother trying to eject the intruders. 'I've got five minutes to spare before I give the lads their team-talk, so why don't you two come along with me to inspect the pitch?'

'Honest?' Jimmy gaped, going weak at the knees.

'Sure, if you're quick.' Kevin led the way into the clubhouse, past the players' changing-rooms, down a corridor and out through the tunnel on to the smoothest stretch of grass Daisy and Jimmy had ever seen.

The turf which rolled out before them was clipped and trimmed and rolled. It was marked out with straight, pure white lines and the pitch was empty except for the ground staff who positioned corner flags and checked the nets.

'Hey, boss,' a man in a yellow tracksuit said as he jogged by, carrying a string-bag bulging with footballs.

'Nice to have you back, boss,' another said, dashing into the clubhouse with a stack of programmes.

'Nice to be back, Charlie.' Kevin greeted them and strolled on ahead of Daisy and Jimmy. He tested the turf with the toe of his shoe, then gazed around the ground at the banks of empty terraces.

In the magic of the moment, Daisy pictured them full. Each stand bursting at the seams with cheering, chanting fans.

'Jimm-mmy Black, Jimm-mmy Black!' Then, 'Dais-ee, Dais-ee, give them their answer, do!' They roared out the old song with special small changes: 'We're half-crazy, all for the love of you!'

Daisy accepted their cheers. She limbered up under dazzling lights, shook hands with the opposition, took up her position in the centre of the pitch. Jimmy was on the right wing, hungry for the ball as usual. The whistle blew. The cup tie had begun...

'What do you say to a short trial right here and now?' good-natured Kevin Crowe invited. He took a ball from one of his staff and rolled it across the grass towards Jimmy.

'Honest?' he gasped again in disbelief. 'Here? Now?'

'Pass to me, Jim!' Daisy cut in eagerly. She jogged on the spot to loosen up, put in a short sprint towards the centre line, then waited for him to tap the ball.

'Dais-ee! Dais-ee!' Sixty thousand people roared her name.

Jimmy overcame his nerves to produce a smart, accurate pass.

Daisy took the ball and ran with it. She swerved around an imaginary defender, then flicked the ball back to Jimmy.

'Steel-ers, Steel-ers, Steel-ers!'

Passing back and forth, Jimmy and Daisy dribbled the full length of the pitch, encouraged by Kevin Crowe, who ran with them until they reached the goalmouth. Then he took up his old position as keeper, crouching low, ready to deflect any shot that flew towards him.

'Offside!' a mob of angry opposition fans

protested as Daisy made the final, unselfish pass. 'Referee!'

'No way was that offside!' Daisy muttered under her breath. 'Go for it, Jimmy; shoot!'

Jimmy swung back his left foot, then booted the ball at the goal. It skimmed the ground like a bullet, slipping under the great Kevin Crowe's grasp and thudding into the back of the net.

'Ye-e-e-es!' *The Steelers'* fans went mad with delight.

Jimmy leaped in the air, then did three forward flips. Daisy ran to embrace him and share the applause.

'Not bad!' Kevin grinned. He stooped to fish the ball out of the back corner. 'Who taught you two to play soccer?'

'Nobody,' Jimmy muttered. 'We just learned in the park.'

'Well, consider your names at the top of the list for the Academy when it opens,' Kevin promised them, glancing at his watch and seeing that he'd run short of time. 'I'm hoping to hold a two-week summer school in July next year, as long as I get the go-ahead from the board of governors to use the Steelers' training ground.'

'Two weeks?' Daisy came down to earth with a bump.

'Yes, that's the plan.' The coach walked them back towards the tunnel. 'We'll be offering fifty places for a fortnight's live-in course during the long holidays.'

'So we'd have to go back to school afterwards?' Jimmy double-checked. Bad news. In fact, major disaster, as far as Daisy's grand running-away plan went.

'Sorry about that.' Kevin laughed at their shocked faces. Then he turned to one side to take out his mobile phone and answer a loud ring. 'Yes, this is Kevin Crowe,' he said, then listened. 'Could you repeat those two names? ...Right, yes, I see. Got that!'

Clicking the off-button, he looked closely at Jimmy and Daisy. 'How about you two joining me in five minutes in the executive suite to talk over your future plans?' he invited.

'Can you believe this?' Jimmy hissed.

They'd got over the shock of learning that their stay at the soccer academy was going to be a short one and decided that they could change their running-away plan to suit the new situation. In any case, they had to concentrate on the moment in hand.

He and Daisy were surrounded by silver trophies and shields. They lined the walls of the posh suite, alongside photographs of the Steelers going back forty or fifty years.

'Do I believe this? No; pinch me to see if I'm awake!' she whispered back.

Wall-to-wall carpet woven in the Steelers' own special two-tone stripes. Squeaky leather armchairs and low glass tables. A wide window with a perfect view of the pitch below.

'Ouch, not that hard!'

'Sorry – not!' Jimmy trotted around the room, heading an imaginary ball. He gave a victory salute to the winners of the 1953 FA Cup Final.

'Kevin Crowe wants to discuss our futures!' Daisy needed to say it out loud, over and over. She checked the clock on the wall. 'He'll meet us here after he's delivered his team talk, which will be in one minute and twenty seconds precisely! How brilliant is that?'

'Yeah!' Jimmy sighed. 'You know all that

stuff he said about working hard at our ball skills and not giving in until we get where we want to be?'

Daisy nodded, one eye on the ticking clock, one eye on the door through which the Great Man would return. 'He was right. And I quote: "Talent alone is never enough. It's the dedication that counts."'

'I'm one hundred per cent dedicated!'

Jimmy swore.

'Me too. Football is my life. Isn't it cool?'

They sighed and each sank into a leather armchair with a squeak and a hiss of air. Then they sat up again as they heard footsteps come up the stairs. Not just one set, but two or three. It sounded to them like Kevin was returning with perhaps a couple of members of the team to add their encouragement.

Maybe even Robbie Exley himself!

They braced themselves as the door opened.

And there, framed by cups and medals, stood Miss Ambler, flanked by Winona Jones and Nathan Moss.

Seven

How? What? When? Where?

How had it all gone so horribly wrong?

What would happen now?

When had Winona and Nathan put two and two together to guess where Jimmy and Daisy had run off to?

Where were the runaways' dreams of glory now?

Burst like a bubble, that's where. Vanished

with a small pop into thin air.

'Don't look so downcast.' Miss Ambler spoke kindly as she advanced towards them. Behind her, Nathan looked wise and serious, while even Winona managed not to smile smugly.

'B-b-but!' was all Jimmy could manage to whisper.

Daisy felt the walls of the Steelers' executive suite tilt and spin. She had to grab on to Jimmy for support.

Miss Rambler-Ambler came towards them offering smiles and sympathy. 'Never mind,' she comforted. 'No one's going to be angry with you for running away. Let's just talk about it, shall we, and try to sort things out.'

No, please! For one awful moment Daisy imagined the teacher putting her arms around her and giving her the sugary hug treatment.

Personally, she preferred the 'Daisy, don't do that!' and 'You're a complete disgrace!' approach.

'Miss, we never ran away!' Jimmy claimed, bravely stepping between Miss Ambler and Daisy. 'What gave you that idea?'

Great thinking, Jim! 'Yeah, Miss, who said anything about running away?' Daisy piped up.

Miss Ambler faltered and took half a pace back. 'Winona?' she said, with a puzzled glance over her shoulder.

'Please, Miss, I heard them planning it outside the playground.' Winona looked worried.

'Ttt-ttt!' Daisy said. 'You heard us mention the Kevin Crowe Academy, fair enough,' she admitted. 'But what gave you the idea that we needed to *run away* to join it?'

'Yeah!' Jimmy was in full flow. He frowned and looked daggers at Nathan. 'Everyone knows you only join up for two weeks during the summer holidays. You don't live there forever!'

Wow, had Jimmy suddenly got good at lying! Daisy felt really proud of him.

Miss Ambler fell for it completely. 'You mean, it's all been a mistake? There was no need for any of this big drama after all?'

Daisy smiled as Winona and Nathan shuffled their feet and coughed uncomfortably. Talk about being wrong-footed and caught in the offside trap!

'Everything sorted?' Kevin Crowe popped his head around the door to check things out. Changed into his tracksuit, he was on his way to take up his position on the pitch, ready for the start of the afternoon's training session.

'Yes, fine thanks!' the teacher said quickly. 'In fact, Mr Crowe, we're sorry to have bothered you with that emergency phone call. It seems that Winona and Nathan may have over-reacted to the situation somewhat in thinking we had a huge crisis on our hands. All that Daisy and Jimmy had in mind was to speak to you about enrolling in the Academy; nothing else.'

Kevin nodded and winked. 'Good. No

problem then.' He beckoned Daisy to the door and held out two small white pieces of paper. 'Tickets for next week's Cup match,' he explained. 'Directors' box. See you there.'

Daisy took the tickets and stammered her thanks.

'And remember, all being well, you're top of the list for the soccer academy next summer!'

Jimmy's skinny frame swelled with pride and pleasure.

Yes! Daisy thought. *Yes! Yes! Yes!*

Then Miss Ambler shepherded them out of the clubhouse, through eager fans hanging hopefully around the gate, to her rusty orange VW Beetle.

Daisy, Jimmy, Nathan and Winona squeezed in and the teacher drove them back to school.

Next to Miss Ambler in the front passenger seat, Nathan let Legs out of his jar and stroked him thoughtfully.

Squashed between Daisy and Jimmy on the back seat, Winona was NOT happy. 'You don't know the full story yet!' she hissed.

But Daisy just waved her cup ticket in Winona's face, then squirmed around to show off Robbie Exley's autograph on the back of her T-shirt.

'And remember, Winona,' Miss Ambler
said sternly as she unloaded them outside
the school gates. 'Check your facts before
you raise the alarm. If we'd called in the
police and informed Daisy and Jimmy's
parents, we'd have caused a terrific amount
of fuss and worry over nothing!'

'Yes, Miss.' Winona clasped her hands in
front of her and bowed her head. It seemed
she had more to say, but for the moment
had decided against it.

So the final score was definitely one-nil to
Jimmy and Daisy.

That is, until they had left school well behind
them and were on their way back home to
Duke Street. Daisy's bag bumped against
her shoulder, Jimmy trotted along beside
her.

Miss Ambler's last words were echoing
inside her head.

*'If we'd called in the police and alerted
Daisy and Jimmy's parents, we'd have*

caused a terrific amount of fuss and worry over nothing.'

'Mum and Dad!' she gasped, stopping dead on the pavement.

It was the middle of the afternoon. Her dramatic farewell note had been sitting in front of the microwave at home for seven whole hours!

Disaster!

'My note!' she moaned to her co-plotter, Jimmy. 'They'll have picked it up and read it. Now we're gonna be in real trouble!'

Daisy Morelli, go to your room! What did we do to deserve this? Why can't you be more like Winona Jones?

'You mean, *you're* gonna be in real trouble!' Jimmy reminded Daisy that *he* hadn't left a note. He got ready his own excuses and slipped away.

'Thanks a lot!' Deserted, Daisy unwillingly opened the door to her place.

'Daisy *mia*!' her dad cried, all smiles from behind the counter of the restaurant. His red

striped apron was covered in white flour, his
face flushed from the heat of the ovens.

'You enjoy yourself with your friend,
Winona, huh? You eat a good lunch at her
place?'

*My friend Winona? Lunch at her place?
What* was *this?*

'Daisy, look at the mess you're in as usual!'
Angie Morelli squeezed between the busy
tables, carrying baby Mia on one hip. She
hustled Daisy into the back kitchen and sat
her down. 'And next time, don't go off
without telling me where you're going!' she
warned. 'It's only thanks to Winona that we
knew what you were up to.'

'How come?' Daisy asked weakly. What
was going on? Why weren't her mum and
dad crazy with worry after reading her note?
What did Winona have to do with anything?

'Well, she was the one who had the sense
to pop in here and let us know where you
were. I hope you thanked Mrs Jones for
giving you lunch and looking after you.'

Her mind still in chaos, Daisy snuck a glance at the microwave. No note.

'Winona also picked up the birthday card for Nathan that you'd forgotten to take with you,' Angie explained calmly, following the direction of Daisy's worried look. 'That was nice of her, wasn't it?'

Daisy mumbled and nodded. *Now* she got it; not only had Winona guessed Jimmy and Daisy's every move, she'd also covered for them at home so as not to worry their parents. She'd even whisked away the tell-tale letter and carried out the whole cover-up perfectly.

Groaning, Daisy sagged forward in her chair. It seemed she owed Winona-Perfecta-Jones more than she could ever repay.

Rats! Rats! Rats!

'Daisy, what on earth...?' Angie Morelli spotted the felt-tip message scrawled on the back of her daughter's T-shirt and read it out loud. '"To Jimmy – with best wishes to a star of the future. Yours, Robbie Exley"!'

As Daisy jumped to
her feet and
backed against
the wall, she
dropped her
bag. Out fell
her toothbrush
and a soggy
Herbie.

'Daisy?' Her mum stooped to pick up the hamster. 'I thought you'd left him in your school drawer...?'

Think fast. Dream up a good excuse.

'Well?' her mum asked.

Fat baby Mia goo-gooed and chortled on her hip. In her chubby fist she held a chewed photo of her big sister, Daisy.

'Well...' Daisy began.

She didn't get any further. Her mum marched up to her and turned her around, re-read the message on her back and immediately ordered her upstairs. 'Take that T-shirt off and put it straight in the washing-machine!' she ordered.

'B-b-but... I can't... It's for Jimmy... it could be worth a fortune!'

'Daisy!' Angie insisted. The tune never changed, it was always exactly the same. 'YOU (*push up the stairs*) ARE (*march through the bedroom door*) A (*stern stare, hands on hips*) DISGRACE!!!'

Look out for more Definitely Daisy
adventures - coming soon!

Just you wait, Winona!
Jenny Oldfield

Winona's a goody goody who sticks like glue
and threatens to ruin Daisy's street cred.
Daisy can't deal with a teacher's pet hanging
around - until classmate Leonie invites her to
convert Winona into one of the gang. It's a
hard challenge - but Daisy's determined to
try...

You must be joking, Jimmy!

Jenny Oldfield

It's school sports day, and Jimmy happens upon his teacher's diary. Daisy expects to learn spicy secrets, but the diary, like Miss Ambler, is DULL! So Daisy 'invents' more exciting entries. Now Jimmy believes that Rambler-Ambler is going out with a soccer superstar. 'No way!' his classmates cry. Can Daisy get them to believe...?

I'd like a little word, Leonie!

Jenny Oldfield

It's **World Book Day** and Daisy's class dress up as book characters. Leonie's really into it – until she sees nerdy Nathan wearing the same outfit as her. But when she messes up an important task for Miss Boring-Snoring, Daisy twigs that their twin cat costumes could be a way out of trouble for golden girl, Leonie...

Not now, Nathan!

Jenny Oldfield

Nerdy Nathan's pet spider has gone missing.
Daisy and the gang carry out a frantic
search, but they fail to find crafty Legs.
Poor Nathan's worried sick. But scatty Miss
Ambler, busy rehearsing for Thursday's
school concert, has no time to waste on a
pesky runaway pet...